To market! To market!

Anushka Ravishankar
Emanuele Scanziani

Tara Publishing

I'm going to the market
With some money in my pocket
My mother's given me a lot of change

To spend it anywhere for
Anything I care for—
Something funny, nice or even strange

I don't know what to get:
A cheap and tiny pet?
A mouse? A fish? A pigeon? Or a cat?

A set of building blocks?
A shiny plastic clock?
A book? A mug? A bucket? Or a hat?

A face-mask, odd and weird?
A false moustache or beard?
A ball? A pot? A basket? Or a bun?

As I think and ponder
I look around and wander
About the market, having lots of fun…

Jangle Jangle Jangle

I'm a bangle-holding stand

Nosy nosy nosy

I'm a posy, I smell grand

I'm a rooster, I can fly

Faster

Faster

Faster

Creeping creeping creeping

I am peeping, I'm a spy

Tutti
tutti
tutti

I'm a fruity
kind of dish

Thumping Thumping Thumping Thumping

I'm a jumping kind of fish

Silly

Silly

Silly

Silly

I'm a chilli sort of sneeze

I am many many me's

Funny funny funny

Funny funny funny

I come back from the market
With the money in my pocket
When my mother asks me: so,
what have you bought?

I give her all the change
And say, Ma, it's very strange
I wonder how it happened...

I forgot!

To Market! To Market!
Copyright © 2007

For the text: Anushka Ravishankar
For the illustrations: Emanuele Scanziani

For this edition:
Tara Publishing Ltd., UK < www.tarabooks.com/uk >
and
Tara Publishing, India < www.tarabooks.com >

Design: Rathna Ramanathan, Minus9 Design
Production: C. Arumugam
Printed in Thailand by Sirivatana Interprint PCL.

ISBN: 978-81-86211-99-1